Cassidy
the Costume
Fairy

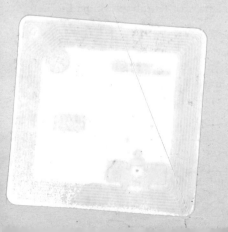

For Lola Jasmine Hart,
with lots of love

No part of this publication may be reproduced, stored in a retrieval system, or transmitted in any form or by any means, electronic, mechanical, photocopying, recording, or otherwise, without written permission of the publisher. For information regarding permission, write to Rainbow Magic Limited c/o HIT Entertainment, 830 South Greenville Avenue, Allen, TX 75002-3320.

ISBN 978-0-545-43391-4

12 11 10 9 8 7 6 5 4 3 2 1   12 13 14 15 16 17/0

Printed in the U.S.A.   40

First Scholastic printing, August 2012

Cassidy
the Costume
Fairy

by Daisy Meadows

SCHOLASTIC INC.

New York Toronto London Auckland

Sydney Mexico City New Delhi Hong Kong

ALEXANDRIA LIBRARY, ALEXANDRIA, VA 2230
ALEXANDRIA, VA 2230

The fairies are planning a magical ball,
With guests of honor and fun for all.
They're expecting a night full of laughter and cheer,
But they'll get a shock when my goblins appear!

Adventures and treats will be things of the past,
And I'll beat those troublesome fairies at last.
My iciest magic will blast through the room
And the world will be plunged into grimness
and gloom!

Contents

Cool Jewels

Kirsty and Rachel walked along the
stone hallway with a group of kids.
They were all chatting excitedly. It
was the second day of their stay at the
Golden Palace, a beautiful mansion
in the countryside. They were having
a wonderful time! The Golden Palace
was amazing—it had been built from
gleaming white stone hundreds of years

ago, and had high towers topped with golden turrets. The owners of the palace were having a special kids' Royal Sleepover Camp during spring break. It included lots of different fun activities. Kirsty and Rachel were staying all week. They loved the fact that they were sleeping in a bedroom with two four-poster beds where real princes and princesses had slept once upon a time!

But that wasn't the only amazing thing about their stay there. Yesterday, the girls had found themselves on a brand-new fairy adventure! This time, they were helping the Princess Fairies look for their magical tiaras. The Princess Fairies were cousins of the king and queen of Fairyland. They had been their special guests at a Fairyland Palace ball, but

Jack Frost and his mischievous goblins
had snuck into the ball—and had stolen
the seven Princess Fairies' tiaras. The
tiaras were full of powerful fairy magic.
Without them, no human or fairy could
have a happy or magical time!

"Follow me, everyone.
Come and see the
palace's Jewel
Chamber," said
Louis, one of
the palace
directors who
was running
the camp.
"Through here."

Kirsty and Rachel
followed the group into
a small wood-paneled room that had

glass display cases along the walls.

"Wow," Kirsty breathed, as she stared into the first case. "Princess Charlotte's christening bracelet from when she was a baby—a gift from the Spanish royal family, over two hundred years ago!"

"And here's a silver helmet that a knight would have worn," Rachel said, gazing into the next case. "This sign says it belonged to a knight named Sir Beaumont, who stayed here in the

eighteenth century." She grinned. "It's so exciting to think about lords and ladies and knights being right here in this palace, isn't it?"

"Okay, everyone," came Louis's voice just as Kirsty was about to reply. "Let's go to the Throne Room next."

The group followed him as he left the Jewel Chamber. Just then, Kirsty and Rachel saw Caroline, another one of the palace directors, carefully locking the door once everyone was out of the room. She put the keys in her pocket and hurried to catch up with the others.

The Throne Room was farther down the hallway. It was a huge room with a high vaulted ceiling, gold-framed oil paintings on the walls, and an enormous red and gold patterned tapestry hanging at one end. In front of the tapestry sat two golden thrones studded with shiny jewels. The thrones' wooden frames were carved with fancy designs.

"Oooh!" gasped some of the kids, and Kirsty and Rachel grinned at each other in delight. Both girls were thinking the same thing — the thrones reminded them of King Oberon's and Queen Titania's thrones in Fairyland!

"Oh, I hope we meet another Princess Fairy today," Rachel whispered to Kirsty, who nodded, feeling tingly at the thought. Their fairy adventures were always so wonderful!

Louis invited the kids to go up in pairs to try out the golden thrones. Rachel was surprised by how small she felt, sitting on the large throne. Kirsty had to wait for a boy wearing big sneakers and a baseball hat pulled low over his face to get off the throne. "Come on, let Kirsty have a turn now," Louis called over, noticing Kirsty waiting patiently. Louis smiled. "I think someone is enjoying being on a throne a little too much!" The boy shuffled off reluctantly, and Kirsty got to sit on the throne next to Rachel. It was very cold and hard. "The kings and queens must have needed cushions if they had to sit on these for very long." She giggled.

"Has everyone had a turn on the thrones? Wonderful," Louis said. "Our next stop is the Costume Gallery—where there's a surprise waiting for you. This way!"

A Dress-Up Mess-Up

Louis and Caroline led the kids to another room that had mannequins dressed as kings, queens, knights, servants, and musicians. There was even a court jester mannequin, complete with a red and yellow hat that had bells on the ends.

In the middle of the room stood a model of the Golden Palace with tiny figurines positioned in the windows, dressed similarly to the mannequins.

Louis called everyone over to see the model, and pointed out the tiny figures taking part in a royal pageant on the palace grounds. "A pageant, if you didn't know, is a display where people dress up to portray scenes from history," he explained.

"And that's what our surprise is," Caroline added. "Today, we're putting on our very own pageant right here at the Golden Palace. The pageant will be open to the public. And the stars of the show are going to be . . . all of you!"

Louis opened a closet door and pulled out a rack full of costumes. "Ta-da!" he said.

Rachel and Kirsty smiled at each other excitedly. This sounded like fun!

Other kids were already begging for the

costumes they wanted. "Can I be a princess?" "Can I be a knight?" "Can I be the king?"

"Whoa!" Caroline laughed, holding up a hand. "It's the luck of the draw." She held up an upside-down jester's hat and showed them that it was full of slips

 of paper. "Take one of these and you'll find out who you're going to be in the pageant," she explained. One by one, the kids took a slip and read it out loud.

"I'm a kitchen maid," one boy cried.

"I'm a lute player," read a girl.

"I'm the king!" said the youngest boy

in the group, looking thrilled—
especially when his big sister pulled out
a slip saying that she was the king's
servant.

When the hat came to Rachel, she
took a slip that said, "You are
a brave knight named
Sir Beaumont
who once helped
save this palace
from a deadly
enemy. He wore a
suit of armor and
carried a sword."

"Great," she said,
passing the hat to
Kirsty. "Sir Beaumont—he was the
knight whose helmet we saw earlier,
wasn't he? He sounds cool to me."

Kirsty plunged her hand into the jester's hat . . . but it was empty. "Oh," she said in dismay. "I don't think there are any slips left."

Caroline took the hat from her and looked inside. "You're absolutely right," she said. "You must be the last one to pick your costume. Which means"—she turned the hat the right way up and plopped it on Kirsty's head—"that you're our court jester! Jesters had the very important job of entertaining the royal family and their guests."

Kirsty beamed.
"Thank you!" she
said, feeling excited.

Kirsty and Rachel
went to find
their costumes.
In addition to the
rack of outfits, there
was also a large
accessory box full of helmets, shoes,
crowns, armor, and all kinds of other
things. Unfortunately, it soon became
clear that although each of the kids
could find part of their costumes, there
were lots of things missing. There were
also items of clothing that didn't seem
to belong there at all—like a witch's
broomstick, an astronaut's helmet, and a
ballerina's tutu.

"This doesn't seem right," Louis said, looking puzzled as he held up a pair of  clown shoes and a robot costume. "I don't remember us having these before. Where are all our knights' swords?"

"I guess we'll have to make do with what we've got," Caroline decided. "Please do your best to put a costume together, kids. We'll come around and help you."

Rachel had a knight's helmet, but no armor or sword. "Maybe this robot costume will work," she said doubtfully.

"It's silver, so I guess it looks kind of like armor." She rummaged through a box of props. "I'll use this broomstick as a sword."

Kirsty, meanwhile, had her hat, but no jester costume. "Jesters are funny," she reasoned, "so maybe I should just wear something silly. . . ." She put on a ballet tutu and some enormous clown shoes, then began looking through a smaller box for something she could use as a jester's stick. She saw something golden shining in one corner of the box and reached farther down to feel around. Was it the golden

bell on the end of a jester's stick?

Something brushed against her skin.
It was so light it tickled! Kirsty blinked
in surprise, then looked down into the
box. With a smile of delight, she realized
that the golden sparkle she'd seen was
coming from a tiny smiling fairy. The

fairy had landed on the palm of her
hand!

Carefully, making sure that nobody
else saw, Kirsty lifted the fairy out of the
box. She quickly took off
her jester hat and placed
the fairy inside, so
she could
stay hidden.
Then Kirsty
hurried to a
quiet corner of
the room and
motioned for Rachel
to come over and see.

"I found some juggling
balls," Rachel said, swinging them in a
bag. "I thought they might be a good
prop for you if you can't find . . . Oh!"

Rachel stopped at the sight of the little
fairy in Kirsty's hat. "Hello!" she said,
smiling.

The fairy had
long dark hair
and was
wearing a pink
chiffon skirt
and a black-
and-white
striped top.
Kirsty and
Rachel had met

all seven of the Princess Fairies
the day before and recognized this
one as Princess Cassidy the Costume
Fairy.

"Hello again," Princess Cassidy
said in a high voice. She raised her

eyebrows at the girls' costumes. "Looks like I got here just in time," she said. "Without my tiara full of costume magic, this pageant — and other events everywhere — will be a disaster!"

An Unusual Princess

"We'll help you find your tiara, Cassidy," Rachel said at once. Then her ears perked up as she heard a loud, pouty voice coming from across the room.

"Where's my tiara? I can't be a princess without a tiara!"

The three friends looked over to see
a boy wearing a pink frilly dress and
a long blond wig. He was rummaging
through a box, bent over so they couldn't
see his face. Then he straightened up and
they heard him mutter, "Well, if there's
not a tiara here, I know somewhere else
I can get one. . . ."

"What enormous feet that boy has," Cassidy said suspiciously, pointing out the large sneakers that poked out from the bottom of the pink dress.

"He's the boy who didn't want to get off the throne earlier," Rachel realized. "What's he doing now?"

The three friends watched as the boy tiptoed up to Caroline. He waited until Caroline was busy adjusting somebody's helmet. Then he reached a hand into her pocket.

Kirsty and Rachel gasped as he pulled out a bunch of keys and snuck away. Just as he was leaving the room, they got a good

glimpse of his face for the first time —
his skin was green. He wasn't a boy at
all — he was a goblin!

"Quick, let's follow him," Rachel
said, and she and Kirsty hurried after the
goblin, with Cassidy peeking
out from Kirsty's
jester hat.
The goblin had
hitched up his
dress and was
scurrying down
the hallway
back toward the
Jewel Chamber.
They saw him use
Caroline's keys to unlock
the door and disappear inside.
"Oh, no," Kirsty whispered in horror.

"He's going to
steal a real tiara
from the jewel
collection!"

"Wait," Cassidy
said as they
approached the
door of the chamber.
"Let me turn you into
fairies and we can all
fly in there without him
seeing us."

There was no one else in the hallway,
so it was safe. Kirsty and Rachel stood
still while Cassidy waved her magic
wand and muttered a few magical-
sounding words. Sparkles circled
around them. In the next moment, the
two girls began shrinking smaller and

smaller until they were the same size as
Cassidy. Now they both had beautiful
shimmering wings on their backs, too.

"Look! Our costumes shrank with us."
Rachel giggled, seeing the now-tiny
broomstick in her hand, and the bag of
juggling balls that Kirsty had thrown
over one shoulder. "Come on, let's see
what he's up to."

The three fairies fluttered silently into
the Jewel Chamber, being careful to fly

high so that they weren't in the goblin's line of sight. Then Cassidy's mouth dropped open in surprise. She pointed at the main display case. "Look!" she whispered urgently. "It's my magic tiara!"

Rachel and Kirsty gazed down at the case. Sure enough, there between a glittering jeweled necklace and a silver bracelet was Cassidy's silver jeweled tiara, gleaming and sparkling against the black velvet background.

The girls all held their breath as the

goblin headed straight for the display case and unlocked the door with another of Caroline's keys. But before he could grab the tiara, a second goblin burst into the room. He was wearing a uniform cap with GUARD written on it.

"Halt!" he sputtered. "Hands off! Jack Frost told me to put the tiara here so that it would be safe from those meddling fairies. I'm not allowed to let anyone near it, not even you."

The princess goblin stomped his foot. "Well, I'm playing Princess Goblina in

the pageant, and I'm telling you, I *need* a tiara!"

The guard and princess goblin started arguing. While they were shouting at each other, Kirsty seized the chance to fly into the open display case. *This is almost too easy,* she thought, smiling. She could take the tiara right from under the goblins' noses! But unfortunately, as she flew inside the case, the bag of juggling balls on her shoulder knocked the silver bracelet off its hook. The bracelet fell to the bottom of the case with a *clunk*.

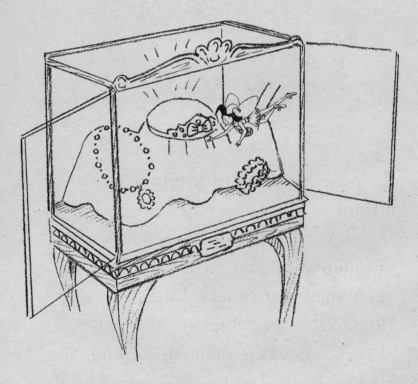

The goblins stopped arguing at once, and Kirsty froze in fright. The princess goblin's eyes gleamed when he saw Kirsty in the case. He snatched the tiara before she could even touch it. Then he slammed the door shut and locked it. Kirsty was trapped!

Sir Beaumont to the Rescue!

Rachel and Cassidy gazed helplessly at each other, then at Kirsty, locked behind the glass door. How could they get her out?

The guard goblin looked startled. He gazed from Kirsty to the tiara and back to Kirsty again, as if he couldn't quite believe his eyes. "You see?" he shouted at the princess goblin. "I *told* you to leave well enough alone. What if there are more fairies around here, trying to steal our tiara?"

Cassidy gritted her teeth. "It's *my* tiara," she said in a tiny, angry whisper.

"We need to find a better hiding place for it," the guard goblin said. "Let me think. . . ."

"How about on my head?" the princess goblin suggested, shoving it on top of his blond locks. "People will think it's part of my costume. Only *we'll* know that it's a real tiara."

The guard goblin looked doubtful. "Well . . . oh, I guess so," he said after a while. "I can't think of a better place right now. But you've got to be careful with it, all right? Come on, let's get out of here before anyone spots us."

And with that, the two goblins left the room. Cassidy's tiara glittered under the spotlights where it sat nestled on the goblin's wig.

Cassidy and Rachel watched them go, then flew down to Kirsty.

Rachel tugged on the glass door,

hoping that the goblin, in his hurry, had not locked it properly, but it didn't move. "Are you all right in there?" she called to her friend.

Kirsty nodded bravely. "I'm fine. Why don't you go after the goblins? We don't want to lose them." Cassidy shook her head. "And leave you here, all alone? No way!" she said. "A true princess would never do something like that. Now let's see if some good old-fashioned fairy magic will open that glass door." She pointed her wand at the

lock and chanted a
complicated spell
under her breath.
Nothing
happened.

Cassidy's shoulders
drooped. "Oh, dear,"
she said. "Without
my tiara, my magic
isn't as strong as usual. How
can we get you out, Kirsty?"

Rachel looked around for inspiration.
There had to be a way to set Kirsty free!
Then she caught sight of her costume
reflected in the glass door. Sir Beaumont
wouldn't ever give up, would he? She
had to think of *something*. . . .

She remembered the broomstick
she was holding. It wasn't exactly a

traditional weapon, but now that it had shrunk, it looked just the right size to fit in the keyhole. "Maybe I could use my broomstick to pick the lock," she said eagerly. "Let me try. . . ."

She pushed the end of the tiny broomstick into the lock and jiggled it a few times. To everyone's delight, the

lock clicked—and the door swung open! "Sir Beaumont to the rescue!" Rachel laughed as Kirsty flew out and hugged her. "Thank you," Kirsty said happily. "Now let's lock up this case again and find those goblins!"

Cassidy flew down and put the silver

bracelet back in place. Then Rachel shut
the glass door and used her broomstick
to lock it again.

The three fairies soared out of the
Jewel Chamber, closing the door behind
them, and flew down the hallway in
search of the goblins.

It wasn't hard to find them. The
goblins were squabbling so loudly that

it was easy to follow the sound of their voices. The three friends flew down a spiral stone staircase and into the Hall of Mirrors—a long rectangular room with mirrors of all shapes and sizes lining the walls. Princess Goblina was admiring his many different reflections. "I look so handsome in this tiara," he said.

The guard goblin scowled. "Hurry up, we need to go. Jack Frost trusted me to look after that tiara. He'll be furious if we don't find a safe place for it," he grumbled.

"Just wait," Princess Goblina snapped. "And stop whining! I've got to make sure it's on properly."

Rachel, Kirsty, and Cassidy flew in quietly, staying close to the ceiling in the hope that the goblins wouldn't notice them. They knew that if Cassidy could get close enough to the princess goblin, she could use magic to change the tiara to fairy-size and take it back.

But before the fairies could get any closer, the guard goblin caught sight of their reflections in one of the mirrors. His eyes widened in alarm and he spun around. "Fairies!" he gasped. "Run, Goblina, run!"

Jest in Time!

The princess goblin scampered out of the room, one hand protectively clutching the tiara on his head. His sneakers slapped against the tiled floor as he ran.

Kirsty, Rachel, and Cassidy tried to fly after him, but the guard goblin swatted at them with his big green hands. "Come here, you pesky fairies," he said, snatching at thin air as he tried to grab them. "You're not getting that tiara—I won't let you!"

The fairies dodged and swerved around the guard's flailing hands. They eventually managed to zoom out of the Hall of Mirrors and chase the princess goblin. They heard his loud footsteps go up the spiral staircase again. Then all went quiet.

"He stopped," Cassidy said in surprise. "Unless he took off his shoes?" Kirsty suddenly remembered how much the goblin had enjoyed sitting on the throne earlier, and how she'd had to wait for him to get up. "I wonder if he went back to the Throne Room," she suggested.

The fairies flew along the hallway
and peeked around the door of the
Throne Room. Sure enough, the goblin
was sitting on the throne once again,
pretending to wave to a crowd of people.

"Good morning,
everyone," they
heard him say
in a high-pitched
voice. "Your
princess is pleased
to see so many
admirers."

Rachel had to
cover her mouth
to stop herself from
giggling.

Kirsty looked thoughtful. "If we can
keep him sitting there long enough,

we might be able to fly above his head and get the tiara," she said. "But we'd need him to be distracted, so he wouldn't notice."

Cassidy nodded. "Yes," she said. "What can we do to make sure he stays on the throne?"

Kirsty reached up to scratch her head, forgetting for a moment that her jester's hat was there. Then she smiled. "I could be a jester," she said. "A real jester, entertaining Princess Goblina!"

"Perfect," Rachel said with a grin. "And while he's watching you, Cassidy and I can grab the tiara!"

They all thought this was a good idea.
Cassidy turned Kirsty back to human-
size and had just enough magic left to
give her a real jester costume. Then
Kirsty strolled out in front of the goblin
while Cassidy and Rachel flew to hide
behind a silk screen.

"Good day,
your highness,"
Kirsty said,
bowing low.
"I am your
court jester, here
to entertain you."

The goblin's eyes
widened with
excitement. "Ooh!
I feel just like a *real* princess now," he

said, clapping his hands together.

Kirsty took out her juggling balls and began juggling. To make things more fun, she purposely threw one ball to bounce off her head, and caught another on her foot. She comically hopped around while still juggling the last two balls in the air.

Just then, the guard goblin rushed in. He opened his mouth to say something to the princess—but burst out laughing when he saw Kirsty's antics. The princess goblin was laughing, too, in a very un-princesslike manner—cackling

and snorting with tears rolling out of
his eyes.

Then Kirsty whipped off her
hat and tossed each ball
into the air. She ran
to catch them in her
hat, skidding
across the
polished floor
and making
funny faces. Once all the
balls were in her hat she
put it on her head . . .
and of course, the balls
fell right out, bouncing in all directions!
Princess Goblina cracked up again,
and the guard goblin was laughing so
hard he had to clutch his sides.
Rachel and Cassidy exchanged

glances. "Let's grab the tiara!" Rachel whispered. "Come on!"

They zoomed through the air toward Princess Goblina, whose shoulders

were shaking with glee. But at the
last moment, the guard goblin spotted
the fairies, and immediately stopped
laughing. "Goblina!" he yelled. "Duck!"

A Perfect Pageant

Princess Goblina looked up in horror, saw the fairies approaching, and ducked out of their way. But clever Rachel remembered she still had her trusty broomstick. Sir Beaumont—or actually, Lady Rachel—to the rescue once again!

She lunged forward, stretching the broomstick out in front of her so she could reach the tiara with its tip. Then she expertly flicked the tiara off the goblin's head and sent it flying through the air. She and Cassidy soared down, catching hold of it seconds before it clattered to the floor. As soon as Cassidy touched the tiara, it shrank to its usual fairy size, and she joyfully placed it on her head.

"Hooray!" she cheered, fluttering high into the air. Colorful sparkles of magic burst all around her. "Oh, that feels so much better!"

Rachel flew up after her, and Kirsty grinned. The plan had worked perfectly!

Meanwhile, the goblins argued about whose fault it was that they'd lost the tiara. Kirsty, Rachel, and Cassidy slipped out of the Throne Room and left them bickering.

Outside, Cassidy waved her wand to turn Rachel back to her ordinary size— and Rachel gasped when she saw that she was now wearing the most fantastic knight costume ever! "Oh, thank you,

Cassidy!" she said, smiling as she flipped up the visor on her gleaming silver helmet. "Even Sir Beaumont would be proud of this outfit, I think."

"Thank *you* so much," Cassidy replied, smiling happily. "Both of you — you were amazing! I'm absolutely thrilled to have my tiara back so that I can use its costume magic again. Your pageant should turn out perfectly this afternoon."

"That's great news," Kirsty said. "I'm glad we could help you, Cassidy."

Cassidy gave each girl a tiny ticklish fairy kiss, then waved good-bye and disappeared in a swirl of sparkling magic. After the last sparkle had faded, the girls went to look for the other kids.

They found them outside with Caroline and Louis on the main lawn in front of the palace.

There was a tent with refreshments, and rows of benches where the parents had gathered to watch. "Look, there's Mom and Dad!" Kirsty said, waving

and smiling at them in the audience.
"Come on, let's ask Caroline what we're
supposed to be doing."

Just then, Louis gave a shout when he saw a large box by the side of the tent. "Hey, guys, I found the missing costume box," he said, a smile spreading across his face. "We've got swords, armor, kitchen maids' outfits, princesses' tiaras. . . . Now we can get you all dressed up properly."

"Thank goodness," Caroline said, helping Louis hand out the props and costumes. "I wonder how that box got down here? It's almost as if it appeared by magic!"

She was laughing, but when Kirsty and

Rachel spotted a few telltale sparkles twinkling around the box, they smiled at each other. Unknown to Caroline and Louis, Cassidy's magic really *had* saved the day. Now the girls could enjoy the pageant, and look forward to helping another fairy tomorrow!

THE PRINCESS FAIRIES

Rachel and Kirsty found Hope's
and Cassidy's tiaras. Now it's time
for them to help

Anya
the Cuddly Creatures Fairy!

Join their next adventure
in this special sneak peek. . . .

Sunshine at the Golden Palace

"Another perfect day!" said Rachel Walker happily. She was standing in the sunshine on the grand entrance steps of the Golden Palace. Rachel's best friend, Kirsty Tate, looked up at the sky and smiled as the bright sunbeams warmed her face.

"It's royal weather for a royal palace!"
Kirsty agreed.

Kirsty and Rachel were staying at
the Golden Palace for a special Royal
Sleepover Camp for kids over spring
vacation. Today, Kirsty's mother was
bringing Kirsty's younger cousin Charlie
to spend the day with them.

"I'm looking forward to showing
Charlie all the amazing places here,"
said Kirsty. "I wonder what he'll like
best. The drawbridge? The moat?"

"Or the petting zoo, the magic
staircases, the dungeons, or the maze,"
said Rachel, counting them off on her
fingers. "There are so many things to
show him, I don't think one day will be
enough!"

"Staying here really does make me feel

like a princess," Kirsty said, gazing out across the palace gardens.

"How about a Princess Fairy?" Rachel asked.

The girls shared a secret smile. They were friends with the fairies who lived in Fairyland, and they often helped them when Jack Frost and his goblins caused trouble. At the moment, the fairies needed their help more than ever before. When the girls had arrived at the Golden Palace, they had been invited to a special ball in Fairyland in honor of the Princess Fairies. But Jack Frost had crashed the party and stolen the princesses' tiaras!

"Jack Frost is so mean," said Kirsty, thinking about the cold-hearted master of the Ice Castle. . . .

RAINBOW magic™

There's Magic in Every Series!

The Rainbow Fairies

The Weather Fairies

The Jewel Fairies

The Pet Fairies

The Fun Day Fairies

The Petal Fairies

The Dance Fairies

The Music Fairies

The Sports Fairies

The Party Fairies

The Ocean Fairies

The Night Fairies

The Magical Animal Fairies

The Princess Fairies

Read them all!

📖 SCHOLASTIC

www.scholastic.com

www.rainbowmagiconline.com

HIT entertainment

RMFAIRY